Phil's heart pounded and his head swam. It couldn't be true! Lil won the contest! She was going to scream with the Screaming Babies! "I didn't win!" Phil cried.

"I guess they wanted somebody prettyful," Lil said.

A sound rose inside Phil's chest. He was angry. "AHHRR! AHHRRRRRRR!"

Rugrats Chapter Books

It Takes TWO!

KLASKY
CSUPO INC.

Based on the TV series *Rugrats*® created by Arlene Klasky, Gabor Csupo,
and Paul Germain as seen on Nickelodeon®

SIMON SPOTLIGHT
An imprint of Simon & Schuster Children's Publishing Division
1230 Avenue of the Americas, New York, New York 10020

Manufactured in the United States of America

First Edition

2 4 6 8 10 9 7 5 3 1

ISBN 0-689-83169-2

Library of Congress Catalog Card Number 00-130565

It Takes TWO!

by Cathy East Dubowski
and Mark Dubowski
illustrated by Joe Schiettino

Simon Spotlight/Nickelodeon

New York   London   Toronto   Sydney   Singapore

Chapter 1

Phil and Lil DeVille watched their mom, Betty, put two pictures in an envelope. One was a picture of Phil, and the other, a picture of Lil.

Phil's picture showed him on one end of a seesaw. Lil's picture showed her on the other end of the same seesaw. They looked exactly alike. That's because Phil and Lil were twins. The only way to tell their pictures apart was to read their names on the back.

"Cross your fingers for good luck, pups," Betty said. She licked the envelope and sealed it shut. "I'm entering you both in a contest to be in a music video with the Screaming Babies. You kids may be on TV!"

Phil and Lil looked at their mom with happy grins.

"That's the look! We're gonna win this contest!" Betty told them. Then she took the envelope outside to the mailbox.

"The Screaming Babies, Phil!" exclaimed Lil. "We're gonna be on TV!"

"Fingers crossed!" Phil barked, holding out his pointer finger.

"For good luck!" Lil said, and she laid her pointer finger across Phil's so they made an X.

Just then a loud noise came from the den. It sounded like a cross between an electric guitar and a chain saw. The

Screaming Babies, Phil and Lil's favorite band, were playing!

The twins charged into the den and flopped down in front of the TV. The Screaming Babies were performing their hit, "Diaper Song," on a music video.

I like to eat
my food from a jar,
I like you, baby,
the way that you are.
Changed my bed,
and my diapers, too.
But nothin's ever gonna change
how I feel, how I feel . . .
about you!

And that's how Phil and Lil had always felt about each other, too. Until one day . . .

Chapter 2

"We hit the jackpot, Didi," Betty chortled. "Lil won a spot on a music video! My baby's gonna be a rock star!"

Betty was in the kitchen at the Pickleses' house. She had brought the twins over to play with Didi's son, Tommy, and his best friend, Chuckie.

"That's great, Betty!" said Didi. She pushed her glasses up on her nose and poured her friend a cup of coffee.

"Tell me all about it!"

"I sent the kids' pictures in to this contest, and they picked Lil to be in a video. They're going to shoot the whole thing right in our backyard," Betty told her.

"What's the name of the band?" Didi asked.

"The Screaming Babies," Betty said. "Isn't that a riot? They want a baby in their video. A *real* screaming baby!"

In the next room Phil and Lil were playing with Tommy, Chuckie, and Tommy's baby brother, Dil. They were setting up wooden blocks. Dozens of them. It was supposed to be a city—the city of "Boss Angeles."

Phil was holding a plastic dinosaur in his hand. It was Reptar, his favorite TV star.

"AHRRRRR!" Phil roared. "Reptar is coming to Boss Angeles!"

"Shh, Phil!" Lil interrupted. All the

babies hushed. "Did you hear that?" She was standing by the doorway to the kitchen. "I won! Mom said I'm gonna be a block star!"

"Wow!" exclaimed Tommy and Chuckie.

"What's a block star?" asked Chuckie.

"Someone who gets to scream with the Screaming Babies on TV," Lil said.

"TV!" Tommy and Chuckie gasped again.

"You're gonna be famous, Lil," Chuckie said.

"And you'll get lotsa money too!" added Tommy.

Phil jumped up and down. "Hey, if Lil won, I won too! Mom gave them my picture."

Phil toddled over to the kitchen doorway. He heard Betty telling Didi more about the video.

"It's too bad Phil's not going to be in the video," Betty said, "but he can watch them film it. Oh, you have to bring Tommy over, and of course Chuckie will be here too. Phil will be really proud of his sister, don't you think?"

Phil's heart pounded and his head swam. It couldn't be true! Lil won the contest! She was going to scream with the Screaming Babies! "I didn't win!" Phil cried.

"I guess they wanted somebody prettyful," Lil said.

A sound rose inside Phil's chest. He was angry. "AHHRR! AHHRRRRRRR!"

Betty looked over with a worried frown on her face. "Phil?" she said. "Are you okay?"

Then she spotted the small plastic toy in his hand. The dinosaur with pointy teeth—Reptar.

Betty grinned. "Oh, you're just pretending to be Reptar, aren't you?" she said. Then both moms growled back playfully and giggled.

"Grrr! Grrr!"

Phil made a mad face. But that just made the women laugh even more.

"Ooh! Look at that mad dinosaur!" Betty said.

Phil stomped away, wagging Reptar in front of him and growling. Tommy, Chuckie, and Lil stared at him.

In the kitchen Betty continued to tell Didi about the contest. "The people at the video company had a contest, and I entered Phil and Lil in the same envelope," she said. "I wanted them both to win!

"Well, the video company thought both pictures were of the same kid! They just happened to see Lil's name on the back of her picture—and that's how she got picked!

"I called 'em back to tell them about Phil, but they said that they absolutely, positively wanted just one baby; two would be too much. Too much! I told them it'd be real cute to have twins, you know, but they said no."

Betty laughed, and then added, "Lil's gonna be getting a lot of extra attention, but I think Phil will be okay. He's a big boy."

From the next room came the sound of angry dinosaur noises and blocks falling as Phil demolished the city of Boss Angeles.

Chapter 3

The next morning Lil took twice as long to brush her teeth. She couldn't stop looking at herself in the mirror. When she came out she was wearing sparkly pink sunglasses.

"Why are you wearin' those?" Phil said. "It's not sunny in the bathroom."

Lil shook her head. "Block stars wear sunglasses all the time—even at bedtime!" she said.

Phil stared at her. Block stars? Sunglasses? Bedtime? "Why?" he asked again.

Lil sighed and began to walk away. Phil pointed his plastic Reptar toy at her and growled. "You're not a big star, Lillian," he said.

"You're just jealous, Philip!" Lil said back. "Jealous 'cause I'm gonna scream with the Screaming Babies."

"It's not fair, Lillian," he told her. "They didn't hear us scream. If they did, I woulda won!"

"Uh-uh, Philip," Lil said. "They still woulda picked me 'cause I'm more prettyful."

Phil stuck his tongue out at Lil. Then in a low voice he said, "I scream better than you. Lots better."

Lil's eyes bulged. "Do not!" she shouted.

"DO TOO!" Phil insisted, even louder.

"DO NO-O-O-O-T!" Lil screamed.

"DO TOO-OO-OO-OO!" Phil screamed at the top of his lungs.

Betty heard the squabbling and ran to the kitchen door. "Okay, pups, break it up," she said. "Look, it's a beautiful day. Let's go play outside."

Chapter 4

In the branches over the tire swing, the birds were singing. Sunlight twinkled on the swing set and slide.

"Hey, Lil," Phil said. "Wanna seesaw?"

Lil rolled her eyes. "Not right now," she said, toddling off in the direction of the slide. "I gots to rest."

Then she stopped long enough to look over her shoulder and wrinkle her nose at him. "Block stars got to look good all the time," she added.

When she got to the slide, she slipped out of her sparkly pink sunglasses and put on a pair of sparkly blue ones. Then she lay down on her back on the slide. Sunlight reflected off the shiny metal surface onto her face and arms and legs.

Phil stomped toward the sandbox. He felt like making a castle and smashing it. It was bad enough that he wasn't going to scream with the Screaming Babies, but he was even madder that Lil was acting like . . . like Angelica, Tommy's mean cousin!

A while later Phil was putting the finishing touches on the bridge over the moat when two faces peeked through the fence along the backyard. It was Tommy and Chuckie.

"What's up, Phil?" Tommy said.

"Nothin'!" Phil barked.

Blam! Phil pounded his fist down in the center of his sand castle.

Tommy and Chuckie crawled under a loose picket in the fence. Chuckie stared sadly at the sand castle ruins. "Are you mad at something?" he asked.

Phil didn't answer. He kept pounding his fist in the sand.

"Why are you mad, Phil?" asked Tommy.

Phil picked up a small plastic shovel and scraped a new moat around the flattened sand castle. "'Cause of Lil!" he finally said. He jabbed a finger toward his sister, who was still lying on the slide.

Tommy and Chuckie looked puzzled. "Why are you mad at Lil?"

"'Cause Lil won the contest. She gets

to scream with the Screaming Babies in their music video," Phil said.

"You scream lots better than Lil, Phil!" Chuckie said.

"Yeah, lots!" Tommy agreed.

"I know," Phil said. "But nobody asked us to scream. They just picked her picture."

"That's not fair!" Chuckie protested.

Tommy scratched his bald head. "They picked her picture? How do you know they didn't pick yours? You guys look the same!"

"I dunno," Phil said.

Then he looked across the yard. Lil was still lying on the slide.

"I coulda been the star," Phil said.

"Hey, maybe you *are* the star. The growed-ups just figured you was Lil," Tommy said.

"Yeah," Chuckie said. "And if you're

Lil, you can be in the video too."

"Well, yeah!" Phil said as his face began to brighten. He was getting an idea. "Growed-ups can't tell us apart . . . and maybe something happens and I can pretend to be Lil. . . ."

Chapter 5

"Hey, what if Lil got the chicken pops?" Tommy asked Phil.

"Yeah, or strapped throat!" Chuckie said. "She wouldn't be able to scream! You could pretend to be Lil and take her place."

"And the growed-ups wouldn't know!" Phil added.

Suddenly Chuckie got nervous. "But if you hafta be in the video, how will you know what you're s'posed to do?"

The boys looked at each other. "I dunno," said Phil. Then he turned to Chuckie. "I know, you can find out for me!"

"Me? Why me?" Chuckie asked.

"'Cause," Phil said.

"She's *your* sister, Phil. Why don't you just ask her?" Chuckie said.

"I don't wanna. I don't want Lil to think I'm thinking about her being a block star. She'll think *I* want to be a block star too!"

"But you do," said Chuckie.

"But I don't want her to know!" Phil cried.

"All you gots to do is find out what she's supposed to scream, Chuckie," Tommy said.

"Yeah," Phil said. "Is it 'MA-MA-AAAAAAH!' or is it 'WANHHHHHHHH!'

or is it somethin' else?"

Chuckie's palms were damp with nervous sweat. He wiped them on his shirt. "Gee, I don't know, guys . . ."

"Just go," Phil said. He gave Chuckie a push.

Chuckie looked over at Lil. He slowly scuffed across the grass toward her.

"How come I always have to do the hard stuff?" he complained. But nobody was listening.

Chapter 6

"You're blocking my sun!" Lil said.

Chuckie frowned. "Huh?"

Lil peeked over her sparkly blue sunglasses. "Oh, it's you, Chuckie," Lil said.

Chuckie was puzzled. "Uh, yeah, it's me, Lil," he said. "Who else would I be?"

Lil smiled. Only it wasn't a friendly smile—it was a pretend-to-be-friendly smile. "What do you want?"

"Uh, uh—I think it's great you're going to be in a video," Chuckie stammered.

"Why, thank you, Chuckie," Lil said.

"Yeah, uh, you'll be great!"

Lil tipped her sunglasses down on her nose and gave him a wink. "I know," she cooed.

Chuckie squirmed. Lil didn't seem like the friend he had known all his life. She seemed weird.

"Uh . . . what are you s'posed to, uh, scream?" Chuckie asked shakily. "In the video? Is it 'MA-MA-AAAAAAH' or is it 'WANHHHHHHHH' or is it—"

Lil laughed as she leaned toward Chuckie and whispered, "Chuckie, all I gots to do is *act natural.*"

"*Act natural?*" Chuckie said. "What does that mean?" He repeated the words slowly. He wanted to make sure he got them right when he reported back to Phil.

"That's what my mom told me," Lil said. "All I gotta do is act natural."

"Oh, uh, thanks, Lil," Chuckie blurted before quickly turning and running off.

Chuckie couldn't wait to tell Phil and Tommy what he had found out!

Chapter 7

"Well? What'd ya find out?" Phil whispered eagerly when he saw Chuckie. He and Tommy had been crouched in the bushes behind the back of Phil's house.

"All she's gotta do," Chuckie whispered back, "is *act natural!*"

"Act natural!" Tommy said. "How do you do that?"

Both he and Chuckie turned to Phil.

"Don't look at me!" Phil said. "All I knowed is it sounds important! We gots to find out what it means."

"How are we gonna do that?" Chuckie asked.

"My mom says when you don't know somethin', you look it up in a big fat book," Phil said. "I think it's called the tick-tionary!"

"Where can we find a tick-tionary?" Chuckie wondered.

"We can ask Angelica," Tommy said.

Phil and Chuckie looked at him. "We can't do that!" Phil cried. "She'll know what we're doing! Then she'll make fun of us, and then she'll tell Lil, and then Lil will tell my mom, and then I'll get in big trouble!"

"Don't worry, Phil," Tommy said, "I'll ask Angelica myself."

Chapter 8

"LIL IS IN A WHAT?" Angelica screamed.

Tommy broke the news to Angelica when she came over. And boy, was she mad. Phil and Chuckie cowered behind Tommy.

"I told you this was a crazy idea," Phil whispered. Chuckie was shaking like a leaf.

Tommy wasn't worried. "Lil's gonna be with the Screaming Babies on TV,

Angelica," he repeated. "Lil's gonna be a big block star."

Angelica pouted and stomped her foot. She did not like that Lil was going to be in a music video with the Screaming Babies! Angelica thought that she should be the star. After all, she was older, and also the most beautiful girl she knew.

"Why didn't I hear about this before?" Angelica demanded. "I coulda sent them my picture! They woulda picked me!"

She paced back and forth with her hands behind her back. "I have to be in that video," Angelica muttered to herself.

After pacing back and forth a few more times, Angelica turned to the babies. "You're going to tell me *everything* you know about this music video," she said. "What's Lil supposed to do in it? Does she have to sing?"

"All she's gotta do," Phil said seriously, "is act natural!"

"What?" Angelica roared. "Act *natural?*" She burst out laughing. "That's all she has to do?"

The babies nodded.

"You stupid babies!" cried Angelica. "I betcha don't know what it means, do you?"

Tommy, Chuckie, and Phil shook their heads.

"It means don't be nervous!" Angelica said with authority.

"Aww!" Phil scowled. Lil hadn't told Chuckie anything important—only that she shouldn't be nervous!

"Now what are we gonna do?" Chuckie moaned. "If Phil doesn't know what to do, he can't pretend to be Lil and be in the video!"

"What did you say?" Angelica glared at Chuckie.

"Uh, nothin'," said Phil.

Angelica stared at them. "Tell me," she demanded.

The boys had to tell her now. They had to tell her that Phil was secretly going to take Lil's part in the video.

"Well?" asked Angelica.

Tommy and Chuckie looked at Phil.

"Uh," Phil began to say, "I was thinking that if something, uh, happens to Lil . . . well, uh, b-because I look like Lil, I could pretend to be Lil, and be in the video—"

"And no one would know the difference!" finished Angelica.

"Yeah!" said Phil with a big grin on his face.

To their surprise Angelica was smiling too.

"So you think something might happen to Lil, huh?" Angelica asked. "And then they might need a new star for the video. . . ."

Angelica fluffed her hair. "Boys, I think this could be the beginning of a beautiful friendship!"

Chapter 9

In no time Angelica found out everything there was to know about the music video shoot.

That was because Angelica knew how to talk to grown-ups. She could get them to do—and tell her—almost anything. Angelica had asked Betty all about the video.

"Gosh, you must be so proud of Lil!" Angelica had cooed to Betty.

Betty was happy that Angelica seemed interested in the music video.

And she had told Angelica *when* Lil was supposed to scream, *how loud* Lil was supposed to scream, and *what* Lil was supposed to scream.

Angelica was delighted. *She* could be in the music video once Lil was out of the way. That was her plan. And it was part of her plan to tell Phil what she knew—but not everything. There were some things Angelica had found out that she was going to keep to herself— like what Lil's costume was going to be.

"Just look at what Lil gets to wear!" Betty had told her. She'd held up a pretty pink dress with lots of ruffles. "I didn't show Lil yet. I want it to be a surprise!"

"She'll look adorable," Angelica had said, picturing Phil in it and trying hard not to laugh.

Angelica was also not going to tell Phil about the lacy bonnet, the pink patent leather shoes, and the pink baby bottle.

"Look," Betty had told her. "In the video, the baby is supposed to drink from a baby bottle. Isn't that sweet?"

"Oh, that'll be really cute," Angelica had said, thinking about Phil all dressed up and sucking on a dumb bottle.

When Angelica got home she went straight to her room and told her doll, Cynthia, everything. "Phil will *never* wear all that girly stuff and drink from a baby bottle!" Angelica said.

She wasn't crazy about drinking from a bottle, either, but there was no question she'd do it to star in a video.

Angelica pumped her fist in the air. "Yes! With Lil *and* Phil out of the way, I can take over! Everyone will see who the real star is!"

Chapter 10

"Quiet on the set!" someone yelled.

BWAANNGGG! wailed a loud electric guitar.

The five members of the Screaming Babies rock band were setting up in Phil and Lil's backyard. They all had hair like Tommy's. They all had glasses like Chuckie's.

And when all their mikes and instruments were plugged in, they were even louder than Angelica.

Chuckie covered his ears. "It's too loud, Tommy! They better be quieter or they're gonna get time-out!"

Tommy, Chuckie, and Phil were sitting in the sandbox watching and waiting for Angelica to tell them what they had to do.

"This is really exciting!" Didi shouted to Howard, Phil and Lil's dad, over the sound of the band's warm-up.

"Yeah, thanks for inviting us!" hollered Stu, Tommy's dad.

The backyard was filled with many neighbors. Everyone was excited to have the Screaming Babies make a music video in their neighborhood. And the music video starred their own Lil DeVille!

What they didn't know was that Lil was practically the only kid in the neighborhood who was not there. Lil and Angelica were both missing.

They were in the pantry area of the DeVilles' kitchen.

"Don't worry about a thing, Lil," Angelica whispered. "You're the star. Just relax and enjoy yourself. I'll let you know when it's time to go outside. Here, have another cookie."

"Thanks, Angelica," Lil said, grabbing three.

Angelica gritted her teeth. It was not easy for her to wait on a stupid baby. But her plan was working. She had waited until no one was looking, then she had told Lil that a big star deserved a big treat—cookies. And now Lil was feasting on them in the pantry, with the door half shut.

"This way you don't have to share with Phil!" Angelica explained.

"Mff. Mff," Lil replied, her mouth full of cookies.

Angelica cackled. Everything was going according to her plan. "You just stay here," she told Lil. "I'll stand guard outside, in case your brother comes around, looking for cookies. Whatever you do, don't come out unless you hear me knock real loud," she said.

But Angelica did not stand guard outside the pantry. She ran outside to finish the rest of her plan.

As Angelica stepped outside, Betty nearly ran her over. "Have you seen Lil?" she asked.

Angelica gave her a blank look.

"Never mind!" said Betty, heading toward the front of the house, away from the video shoot.

Angelica dashed over to Tommy, Chuckie, and Phil. "Now's our chance!"

Angelica whispered to the babies. She dragged Phil out of the sandbox. Then she shoved him toward a lady dressed all in black.

"Here she is! Here she is!" crowed the lady. She grabbed Phil's arm. "Come on, sweetie!"

They hoisted Phil onto a table. It only took a minute for her to get him out of his clothes and into the outfit Lil was supposed to wear in the video.

Angelica grinned. Everything was going according to plan! She waited for Phil to have a tantrum about having to wear a pink ruffly dress, a bonnet, and a pair of pink shoes. And she would be right there when they needed a new star!

Tommy and Chuckie toddled up to the table.

"How do I look?" Phil said, fluffing the

lace around the bottom of his skirt.

Tommy and Chuckie looked at each other and shrugged.

"You look like Lil," Chuckie said.

Phil growled.

"Now you look like Phil," Tommy reassured him.

Then the lady in black handed Phil a baby bottle. He put the rubber bulb in his mouth and turned the bottle up. A few seconds later, he slammed it down.

Angelica couldn't believe it. Phil didn't care about the dress. He didn't care about the baby bottle. He was ruining everything!

"Quiet on the set!" a man yelled.

The video shoot was about to begin.

"Camera!"

Cameras scanned the backyard.

"Action!"

The Screaming Babies raised their

instruments in the air. Everyone held their breath, ready for a noisy roar from the band.

But the sound they heard next was not a *BWANGGGGGGGG!*

It was a "WANHHHHHHHH!"

It was the terrifying howl of a very angry Lil.

Chapter 11

Lil screamed at the top of her lungs and ran toward Phil. Betty had found her in the pantry. Lil's face was covered with cookie crumbs.

The sound of her scream had stopped the Screaming Babies and their video shoot dead in their tracks. They'd never heard a sound like that before—not until Phil started screaming too!

Some people covered their ears, but

the Screaming Babies loved the sound of Phil and Lil's screams.

"Is anybody getting this on tape?" shouted the lead guitar player.

The sound crew for the Screaming Babies surrounded Phil and Lil with mikes.

"No one told us there were *two* of them!" yelled the drummer.

Phil and Lil kept crying and screaming up a storm. Then they saw all the people gathered around them. Suddenly Phil winked at Lil. Lil winked back. The twins started laughing and screaming together. This was fun!

The Screaming Babies and the video film crew were enjoying it too. "I say we put 'em in the video together," yelled the singer.

Suddenly the twins stopped screaming. Lil gasped. Phil's eyes bulged.

"Oh, I'm so proud!" Betty squealed.

The sound crew left the twins alone for a moment while they worked with the band. As everyone watched the Screaming Babies play, Lil whispered to Phil, "I'm sorry I was mean. You're the best brother in the whole world!"

"And I'm sorry I was mad at you," Phil said. "You're the bestest sister."

"We shoulda knowed we was better together," Lil said.

"Like always," Phil agreed. "Only . . ."

"What?" Lil asked.

"How about you wear the dress?" Phil suggested. "It's too scratchy for me."

"Okay!" Lil said.

Then the twins were given the cue to start screaming.

"AHHHHHHHH!" But it wasn't Phil and Lil screaming. It was Angelica. She couldn't believe it! Thanks to her, both

Phil and Lil were going to be in the video!

"AHHHHHHHH!" she screamed again. "AHHHHHHHH AHHHHHHHH!"

But no one could hear her. The band was playing now, and anyway, Phil and Lil were *twice* as loud.

About the Authors

Cathy East Dubowski and Mark Dubowski are a husband-and-wife writing team.

Mark says, "I'll start to say something..."

"And I'll finish it," Cathy says.

Just like Phil and Lil. (Except for the diapers.)

Over the years Cathy and Mark have written and illustrated dozens of books, including many featuring licensed characters. They work in a pair of old barns near their home in Chapel Hill, North Carolina, where they live with their daughters, Lauren and Megan, and their two golden retrievers, Macdougal and Morgan.